Pretty Poppy Pinto played with Princess Pippen.
They wandered to the farmyard and ran around the chickens.
The chickens clucked and fluffed and puffed as they began to huff.
"You're making such a mess," they said, "that really is enough!"

Poppy and Pippen laughed as they ran away.
They were trying to be good, but this was a naughty day.
They splashed a muddy puddle sending the gloop high into the sky.
It landed with a mighty smack on Mr Piggie in his sty.

Mr Piggie grunted and shook his double chins.
He peered through his muddy mask at the two cheeky grins.
"I know I like a mud bath as much as any pig, but I'd rather make one by myself. I really love to dig."

"Over here! Over here!" the sheep began to bleat.
"We want to play, we want to play, it would be a lovely treat."
Poppy and Pippen weren't very sure.
The sheep couldn't be trusted, they were very immature.

Poppy looked over the gate and into the crowded pen. All the sheep were looking back: one, two, three, four, five, six, seven, eight, nine, ten.

"What game do you want to play?" Poppy asked the blinking sheep.

The sheep giggled and laughed, "How about Hide and Seek?"

Poppy looked at Pippen and they both shook their heads.

"We don't know how to play that, do we run around the sheds?"

"Let us out, let us out, we'll show you how to play."
The sheep already knew that this was a naughty day.
Poppy lifted the latch that locked the sheep pen gate.
She realised her mistake, but by then it was too late!

The sheep rushed and pushed and pushed as they all tumbled out.
They scattered all around the farm – they were gone, there was no doubt!
"Come back, come back!" Poppy shouted as she watched their fluffy tails.
But all the sheep were gone leaving nothing but their trails.

"Pippen, oh Pippen, they are such naughty sheep!"
"We are in big trouble and we are in so deep!"
"We have to find them quickly," Pippen said with resolve.
"I agree," said Poppy, "but be careful who we involve."

Poppy Pinto and Pippen looked around for help.
They ran to Mr Piggie and Pippen let out a yelp!
"The sheep are gone, the sheep are gone, they ran off everywhere."
Mr Piggie grunted and grinned. "I bet you got a scare.
You need to find the perfect person for this tricky job.
Why don't you ask Merri the working sheep dog?"

They trotted to the kennel where Merri lay asleep.
"Oh Mr Merri, Mr Merri, help us find the sheep?"
Merri opened his eyes and yawned himself awake.
"Did they trick you to let them out? You've made a big mistake."

Merri jumped up to his feet and quickly sniffed the air.
"I know they're hiding on the farm and I'm sure I know where."
The three friends trotted off in search of the naughty sheep.
Poppy began to think she didn't like playing Hide and Seek.

"Found you!" yelled Pippen as she nudged the ball of wool.
"Get back into your pen, we are not a bunch of fools."
The sheep ran into the pen and they began to chew.
"How many do we have?" Poppy said. They counted, "One, two."

Pippen guarded the pen and Poppy found two more.
"There we go!" said Merri, "That makes one, two, three, four."
Poppy galloped across the farm wise to the sheep's tricks.
She chased two back into the pen.
"That's one, two, three, four, five, six!"

Merri winked and said, “Well done!” He ran out of the gate.
There was a clatter of hooves and a flash of wool.
“That’s one, two, three, four, five, six, seven, eight!”

That only left two sheep to find as Poppy trotted away.
She searched the barn, behind the tree and in the pile of hay.
The naughty sheep watched her from their hiding places.
Can you see them under the cart, can you see their naughty faces?

"Found you!" Poppy yelled triumphantly as she chased them all out.
They tried to run but Pippen helped as they galloped all about.
Merri barked, "That is enough, now back into your pen."
The sheep sighed and trotted home. "That's one, two, three, four,
five, six, seven, eight, nine, ten."

Later that night, Poppy, Merri and Pippen lay tired in their beds.
They yawned and sighed and fell asleep, counting sheep in their heads.
Can you count with them? One, two, three, four....

Milton Keynes UK
Ingram Content Group UK Ltd.
UKHW050853020924
447772UK00003B/30
9781914560927